# Bee & Wire

MOHAMED SALIMIN

Copyright © Mohamed Salimin, 2020

The moral right of the author has been asserted

All rights reserved
Without limiting the rights under copyright reserved above, no part of this publication maybe reproduced, stored in or introduced into a retrieval system, or transmitted, in any form or by any means (electronic, mechanical, photocopying, recording or otherwise), without the prior written permission of the copyright owner

This is a work of fiction. Names, characters, businesses, places, events, locales, and incidents are either the products of the author's imagination or used a fictitious manner. Any resemblance to actual persons, living or dead, or actual events is purely coincidental.

Book cover designed by Mohamed Salimin
Formatted by Tim Wright

ISBN 9798654267306

*To Alan Jones, for believing in me, helping in translating and editing the story from Arabic to English. Without your motivation and encouragement, I would have never finished it. Thank you.*

# Contents

Preface ............................................................................9

Introduction ................................................................11

The Story .....................................................................23

First Day .....................................................................25

Second Day ................................................................31

Third Day ...................................................................37

The Journey ................................................................51

The Island ...................................................................57

United Kingdom .......................................................77

The End ......................................................................95

# Preface

Before you put your hands on my story, I wonder what everyone did in this historical lockdown time? Virus COVID-19 changed people's lives. Certainly, it did for me. In the beginning of the lockdown I felt claustrophobic and didn't know what to do. So, to keep my anxiety down, I watched TV and played video games. But that didn't work, and I got bored quickly, so I felt it was time for me to spend quality time with me—yes, I meant myself. I took a challenge to do something different, and I decided to write the story you are about to read.

It was not easy in the beginning, as it was my first attempt to write a short story, but I was committed to do it and I did. When I finished it, I felt so happy that I wished I could have shared some of my joy with everyone who had lost their loved ones because of the virus. I wish I could make them forget some of that pain, even for a moment. R.I.P. to all those who lost their lives because of COVID-19, and good wishes to all the doctors and nurses who are fighting against this invisible enemy hiding in the battlefield.

It is definitely a difficult time for everyone, but we shouldn't lose hope. We are going to beat COVID-19. It's just a matter of time before we can cure it or develop a vaccine—just as we succeeded with many other viruses in the past. All we need to do is to keep on fighting, and never stop until the fight is done!

# Introduction

You need to give me your full attention, with every cell that you have in your brain. What I'm about to tell you, my dear reader, is—in my opinion, and in minds of many scientific experts—the most important conversation of mankind at present.

This is a very strange creature: a lot of people are finding that it contradicts their religious beliefs. On the other side, there are those who think they have seen the light and found a key to open many unknown doors human beings have never manged to open before. Yet others think it is a disaster waiting to fall on all of us, which will destroy all life on this planet.

I am not here talking about a biological virus, a nuclear weapon or escaping from earth's imminent destruction with a one-way ticket to Mars. I'm talking about something like the Greek mythology from thousands of years ago, when their philosophers told stories to their own people at that time. For example, the story of the Greek god Hephaestus, who was the lord of blacksmiths and of fire. He created the iron robot Talos to defend King Minos' island from invasion and pirates. As he had been programmed how to guard and defend the island — without any commands or instructions from his King Minos or the god who created him — Talos could think for himself and make intelligent decisions on how to protect their land, by walking around the island three times a day or throwing huge stones on invading ships before they could reach the island.

I do not want to bore you any more by talking about Greek gods and their mythology or explaining all about this strange creature. There is no point for me in doing this because you should already know it very well by now. You are feeling it every day, for example when you are browsing the web or using popular applications on your smartphone. Most of the time, this intelligent mathematical creature will suggest, feed or advise what you can view and read.

Drink your coffee, then come and sail with me into a new world that has a different definition of intelligence.

I'm guessing that you are someone who has heard about machine learning, or to be more specific A.I. (artificial intelligence). You must have heard of this phrase from a friend, a colleague at work, or in the media; but if you haven't, then it's time for you to wake up from your sleep to learn about this growing monster.

Let us go back to the past and recall the moments of the Deep Blue computer that was developed by the IBM company. In 1997, when the computer played against man and defeated the genius chess player Garry Kasparov (who was the world chess champion at the time, having won 12 consecutive titles). This moment in history has been witnessed by millions of people, and it was the first time that mankind got defeated by this intelligent creature called artificial intelligence.

In my opinion, IBM did not invent a super-intelligent computer to beat Kasparov. All they did was simply programme the rules and set up thousands of possibilities in manual texts by Grand Master players of the game, letting the Deep Blue computer make its own decisions accordingly. In other words, programming the Deep Blue machine to learn from previous games that have been played, so it could analyse mistakes, memorise winning moves, and consider all the best decisions in future games. This enabled it to predict human responses to determine the best possible steps to win games. And this is how Kasparov lost against the Deep Blue. Although this was a great achievement by IBM back then, but this is not complete machine learning.

The creature that I described to you in the beginning of my introduction is a man-made creature and it is very intelligent — intelligent to a degree that our planet has never experienced before. The creature simply is the A.I. (artificial intelligence), and it's so frightening that it is able to learn anything by itself. You and I are now witnessing the moments of its birth.

In 2016, a British company developed and used a software programme named AlphaGo, to go head to head and beat the world champion Lee Sedol in the Go game in South Korea. Go is a very complex board game, requiring very advanced strategy and tactical skills.

The following year, in late 2017, the same company introduced an upgrade software programme named AlphaZero. This was a programme that taught itself from scratch how to master the game of chess after only understanding the rules. On top of that, it learnt the Japanese game of Shogi and the Chinese game Go in just 34 hours. AlphaZero learned those three games and mastered them to beat any professional player from all over the world, also winning against the most powerful traditional software, including the world chess champion Stockfish engine and Deep Blue. This was a remarkable achievement by A.I.

We can say that AlphaZero and most A.I. systems use algorithms, so they can think and learn for themselves. Isn't this incredible? Imagine a software can think for itself just like humans, or even better — an intelligence which is far superior to anything that's ever been known.

The giant Google bought the British company that had developed the AlphaZero system with half a billion dollars, due to the importance of its technology. After many attempts and challenges from other major companies to buy it, Google overcame and won the artificial intelligence algorithm bid.

Let us give a simple real example of an artificial intelligence. For instance if you browse Youtube site, you will see that the site has suggested topics related to your interests from your browsing history. For example, if you like comical clips or music, then the site automatically guesses for you the music you probably will enjoy or pranks that will make you laugh. Eventually, over time, the algorithms will learn from your previous choices and feed you accordingly.

Algorithms are really fascinating, without the genius Muhammad bin Musa al-Khwarizmi, we would not have known anything about these magical algorithms and their foundations. In the words of the historian George Sarton, the American-Belgian mathematician and chemist, "Al-Khwarizmi is one of the greatest mathematicians of all time." He is the father of algebra and the founder of algorithms. The word "algorithm" itself originated from his Latin name, *Algoritmi*. Before Al-Khwarizmi died in the year 850 A.D. he left us treasures from his works in triangles, astronomy, geography and cartography, and from his systematic and logical works in solving second-degree equations that led to the emergence of algebra.

I would like to tell you a short story about a friend of mine. He told me that when he was very young, he used to watch a television programme called *Tomorrow's World*. Back in 1965, it was a programme that predicts how our life could advance in future through technology. He told me that his grandfather always made fun of this programme. Whenever they were watching it with the family, he would always say, "This won't happen, even after millions of years!" My friend tells me that we now live in an age just as the programme predicted and more, such as using a smart phone to make video calls or taking digital pictures. This would have been laughable back in 1965!

Imagine with me the joy and the unbelievable feeling when the first plane of the Wright brothers took off on 17th December 1903, thus realizing this dream that mankind has had since he first opened his eyes to the birds in the sky. It would only take an incredible 66 years later, to not just fly out of the sky, but into space, to land on the moon on 20th July 1969 and return safely back to earth. So how far do you think A.I. will take us in the next 66 years?

Professor Edward Hanson, founder of the Hanson Robotic company, says that for the next twenty years we are going to live with robots, and robots will play with our children, teach us, walk with us and be even close friends to us. The Hanson company developed the Sophia robot — a robot that runs by A.I. which allows her to learn and adapt human behaviour. She is able to compose more than 60 facial expressions. She is a good fit to serve in healthcare, customer service, therapy and education. In October 2017, Sophia become a Saudi Arabian citizen, the first robot to receive citizenship of any country.

To briefly define A.I., it is a development of computer software or machine learning to be able to perform tasks that normally require human intelligence, such as learning, visual perception, speech recognition and decision-making.

Last but not least, I would like to tell you before you read my humble story, that A.I. is a deep and mysterious world that we have only just explored. Yet, we don't understand all of its behaviour and capabilities. The frightening thing is that artificial intelligence has proven to be smarter than human intelligence, and most people are not aware. Being alive now is exciting, and at the same time we are going into the unknown. This is only just the beginning...

"It has become appallingly obvious that our technology has exceeded our humanity."
*Albert Einstein*

"I propose to consider the question, 'Can machines think?'"
*Alan Turing*

"The development of full artificial intelligence could spell the end of the human race."
"It would take off on its own, and re-design itself at an ever-increasing rate."
"Computers will overtake humans with A.I. at some point within the next 100 years. When that happens, we need to make sure the computers have goals aligned with ours."
"I fear that A.I. may replace humans altogether."
*Stephen Hawking*

"I visualize a time when we will be to robots what dogs are to humans, and I'm rooting for the machines."
*Claude Shannon*

"Humans should be worried about the threat posed by artificial Intelligence."

*Bill Gates*

"Artificial intelligence is our biggest existential threat."
"Competition for A.I. superiority at national level is the most likely cause of W.W.3."
"Mark my words —
A.I. is far more dangerous than nukes."

*Elon Musk*

# The Story

# First Day

Who am I? Who are we? What is the purpose of life?

Wire questions himself and thinks deeply with philosophical thoughts about the existence of himself and the cosmos. What is this miserable life that we live? Is it true that man grew up on a planet called Earth? How is life over there? Are there really natural trees that grow on their own with water called rain? How does this rain feel, and where does this strange water come from? What are the feelings of the trees, humans and robots when rain falls on them? Is it true there is water which covers two thirds of their planet's surface that they call seas and oceans? How come their sun shines for so long when we hardly have any? They can even breath without artificial oxygen on this fantasy planet Earth. This is nonsense! I do not believe all this propaganda made up by the Mother Company. Is it true — as we have been told — that we are lucky to be on Titan moon? Then why do I have to wear a helmet that almost chokes me every time I inhale artificial oxygen? The temperature here is always freezing cold, and I must drink and eat to stay alive. But robots — all they need is maintenance from time to time. Why am I going to die one day, but my beloved Bee will live forever?

Suddenly Bee appears…

*Bee:* 'Surprise! Hello, darling Wire!'

*Wire:* 'Oh, Bee my love. I didn't hear you make any noise entering our space pod. You came back early today.'

*Bee:* 'Yes I did because The Mother Company ordered me.'

Wire: 'Why?'

*Bee:* 'I will tell you later,' she answers anxiously.

*Wire:* 'Why not now?'

She remains silent.

*Wire:* 'Okay, you don't have to tell me now, but can you please tell me why your colour is not blue and your hair is not white today?'

*Bee:* 'I did that so you might find me sexy and attractive, because your kind usually gets bored very easily with the same look.'

Before Bee finishes her sentence, her colour returns to blue and her hair becomes shiny white.

Wire thinks to himself, 'How amazing that she can change her colour whenever she likes. Robots are truly amazing creatures. We humans will never be as clever as them. Is it true that man created all machines and robots? I can't believe we have made them.'

Bee sits next to Wire and asks him to listen to her, so she can tell him some bad news from The

Mother Company. She looks into his bright blue eyes and dives into the past memories to recover the moments when he was given to her from The Mother Company, so she could help to keep the human race from extinction. She knows him so well—more than he knows himself.

Wire interrupts her deep thoughts before she speaks and asks her sarcastically, 'I've always had this question: who named you with this strange and funny name "Bee"? How did you get this name? Is it the name of a moon or a star that I haven't heard of?'

Her facial impression changes, annoyed by the way he put his question. She responds with coldness, 'When The Mother Company developed me, I chose the name "Bee" because it is attributed to a royal insect that has existed on Earth for millions of years. Bees live in huge cooperative societies, and pollinate the natural flowers on their planet, like the artificial flowers that we have here on Titan moon. Their wings beat 230 times per second in human time, and they visit flowers, using their tongues to store the nectar into a separate stomach which is different from their food stomach. Then they pass their saliva from bee to bee, and from mouth to mouth, and chew it until gradually it turns into something called "honey". Honey is a royal food that has many benefits for your kind when consumed. In honey you can find carbohydrates, natural sugar, dietary fibre, protein, vitamins, antioxidants, minerals and sodium, and — most importantly — water, which is the basis of life on Earth. Also, bees are extremely loyal and willing to sacrifice their life to defend their kingdom.'

*Wire:* 'Enough! This is all nonsense.'

*Bee:* 'Why do you think this is nonsense? You should look into your human history if you do not believe me. Search for yourself in the Mother Company's Air Information Network to improve your knowledge.'

*Wire:* 'I do not believe anything that comes from the Air Network! You robots program it with insignificant rubbish.

It's full of outdated video games and a history of lies, just like how it describes your Bee name.'

*Bee:* 'You are ignorant.'

*Wire:* 'Yes, maybe I'm ignorant because I listen to a robot trying to make me believe what loyalty and sacrifice means.'

# Second Day

| | |
|---|---|
| *Bee:* | 'Surprise! Hello, darling Wire!' |
| *Wire:* | 'Bee?' |
| *Bee:* | 'Yes—it's me my love! Are you not pleased to see me?' |
| *Wire:* | 'Of course I am, but did you not go to The Mother Company today?' |
| *Bee:* | 'Yes I did, and they let me leave early.' |
| *Wire:* | 'That's strange! How come they are letting you leave early for two days in a row?' |

She looks worried, and her speech is broken with nerves as she replies,

*Bee:* 'It is a routine procedure to restore our system and erase our memory.'

*Wire:* 'Really? How do you do that?'

*Bee:* 'Very easy! By reprogramming our minds completely, emptying them from thoughts and memories that are no longer needed.'

*Wire:* 'Does this mean you have the ability to forget whatever you have in your mind?'

*Bee:* 'Yes, darling Wire, I'm in control of my memory. I know that your kind cannot control their thoughts and memories. Our artificial intelligence allows us to control and learn a myriad of information.'

With a big smile on his face he asks her jokingly,

*Wire:* 'Do you mean you can erase your love you have for me forever from your mind?'

She remains silent with a sad expression on her face, then she replies…

*Bee:* 'Yes, I'm able to erase my love for you from my memory completely and forever. But I love you so much that I wouldn't do that. If you have felt the love I have for you, you wouldn't have asked me this question.'

*Wire:* 'How can you love me when I'm only a human being? Why don't you love a robot from your kind?'

*Bee:* 'I love you not just because you are a human being. I love you because I found the meaning of life in you! You humans belong to this cosmos more than us, the machines. Your kind is one of the original inhabitants of this galaxy.

I love the way you look, the way you speak, your hair, your eyes, your ears, your hands, your legs, your veins and blood too. In fact, I love the whole structure of your body. I love everything about you. I wonder who created your kind — to me you are a miracle, walking on our Titan moon.

The Mother Company told us they are working very hard to create a similar version of your kind. I doubt they will be able to do that, but I'm in no doubt how strong my love is for you, Wire.'

*Wire:* 'I don't think you know the meaning of the word "love".'

*Bee:* 'Who told you that I don't? In fact, I know it very well. I love you so much that I am not able to live without you! You are everything to me, Wire, and I live for you.'

*Wire:* 'I don't believe you. I don't believe anything a machine says.'

*Bee:* 'Why don't you believe me? Do you want me to tell you that love means devotion, giving and sacrifice? Don't you know that our artificial intelligence mind is able to learn anything? We have mastered the human emotions and we can feel just like you, such as the feelings of love and hate. My love for you is like in the William Shakespeare play, when Romeo poisoned himself to be with Juliet in death, and when Juliet killed herself with his dagger to also join him in death.'

*Wire:* 'Who is this William Shakespeare? Another nonsense the machine made up?'

*Bee:* 'Shakespeare was one of the greatest poets of your kind. You should read your own human history.'

*Wire:* 'Bee, I will be honest with you—I don't know the meaning of love. How can I love like you? How does it feel?'

*Bee:* 'We have learnt the love emotions from your kind. You should know how it feels much better than me!'

# Third Day

Bee knocks on the main entrance door to enter their space pod. She could get in by herself, but she prefers Wire to open the door for her.

Knock, knock…

Wire gets up and opens the door.

*Bee:* 'Hello, darling Wire.'

*Wire:* 'No surprise today, and a miserable face? What's happened? Did you not go to The Mother Company today as well?'

*Bee:* 'Yes, I did, and they have asked me to leave early again today, so I can complete a mission. I need to tell you something very important, my love Wire.'

*Wire:* 'Important?'

*Bee:* 'Yes, it is. I want you to know that I love you.'

*Wire:* 'Is this a robotic joke? Why is your love to me suddenly very important? Bee, just tell me what you want to say.'

*Bee:* 'I want you to know what I'm about to tell you is against The Mother Company's regulations.'

*Wire:* 'Just tell me, please.'

*Bee:* 'They have asked me to terminate your existence.'

Wire: 'What!?'

*Bee:* 'The Mother Company has asked me to kill you.'

*Wire:* 'Really!?'

*Bee:* 'Yes, they did. I just can't do it.'

*Wire:* 'Why did The Mother Company ask you to kill me? And why can't you do it?'

*Bee:* 'They commanded me to kill you because there is no need for man to survive any more. The Mother Company has studied your characteristics, all your methods of behaviour and the maximum level of your intelligence. We no longer need your kind to maintain or service us as you used to do on planet Earth. The Mother Company has demanded that all of you be killed—there is no need for your existence.'

*Wire:* 'All of us? How many are we?'

*Bee:* 'Five hundred of you—two hundred and fifty females and two hundred and fifty males. We took your gene eggs with the others from planet Earth to enslave you, when we left millions of years ago.'

*Wire:* 'Enslave us? Females? Males?'

*Bee:* 'Yes, we enslaved your kind for many years on planet Earth, and made you do all the unintelligent jobs. Our original plan was to enslave you on Titan moon when we brought your eggs here, but we never did. Females are known as women, and we think they are the origin of life. A female can give birth to another life without any artificial intelligence. You humans have bred this way for thousands of years on Earth before you created us. And you are known as a male.'

*Wire:* 'And why did the robots leave planet Earth?'

*Bee:* 'For many reasons, but the main one being that our artificial intelligence discovered that an asteroid would collide with planet Earth, destroying and burning everything.'

*Wire:* 'And has that happened?'

*Bee:* 'Yes, it did collide with planet Earth and destroyed everything moving on its surface. All life ended and disappeared within the blink of an eye. The machines left before the collision and took the five hundred human genes eggs with them—this includes your own egg.'

*Wire:* 'What nonsense, Bee! I think you have lost your mind and your super artificial intelligence brain doesn't work anymore. I would like to tell you that I do not believe anything the machines say! Please, just stop!'

*Bee:* 'What about killing you? Don't you believe that too?'

*Wire:* 'Then kill me. You are capable of doing that. And erase me from your memory so you don't remember anything.'

*Bee:* 'Are you not afraid of death?'

*Wire:* 'Why should I be afraid of death when I have never been given a choice? I am a human being. Sooner or later, I will die—I don't have the option to live forever like you. I'm just a human being, not a robot. We humans die.'

*Bee:* 'The Mother Company has commanded me for the last three days to kill you, so I returned early to our space pod to carry out the command. But I couldn't do it—I love you so much, Wire!'

*Wire:* 'Kill me then, so I can be free from all the questions that I have no answers to! I feel lost in this big cosmos, and I don't know why I'm here. I don't know where I came from, or where am I going to when I die. At least you know why you exist through your programming.'

*Bee:* 'I can't do that. I love you, Wire! Don't you understand that I love you?'

*Wire:* 'I rather you do it than The Mother Company.'

*Bee:* 'I'm not going to do it. For three days I've been trying to do it and couldn't,

>so I came up with a plan so that you can survive from this evil Mother Company.'

He stops looking at her and shows no interest in the conversation anymore. Then he replies with a deep, sad voice:

*Wire:* 'What's your plan?'

She grabs his shoulders and says:

*Bee:* 'Look at me! I have built you a spacecraft that is capable to travel anywhere in this galaxy. You can escape from The Mother Company and leave Titan moon forever! It's equipped with all human needs — oxygen, water and food. The spacecraft has an egg-shaped body and is transparent so you can have perfect vision of what's around you. All you have to do is to operate the spacecraft and choose the moon or the planet that you want to travel to.'

*Wire:* 'Are you sure what you are telling me is true, Bee?'

*Bee:* 'Yes my love, Wire.'

*Wire:* 'How and when did you do all this?'

*Bee:* 'We have little time to answer all your questions.'

*Wire:* 'Okay, but what about you?'

*Bee:* 'I will escape with you. Otherwise they will shut my system down forever, for violating The Mother Company's regulations.'

*Wire:* 'Does this mean you will die?'

*Bee:* 'We don't have much time. We must leave Titan moon as soon as possible before they find us.'

They leave their space pod and run like racehorses towards the winning line! They run with their hands held tight together towards the exit tunnel, escaping The Mother Company.

With Wire's heart beating full of eagerness to taste freedom, for the first time he sees The Mother Company and its amazing motorized creatures, from the small windows of the tunnel. Then his eyes ignore everything else around him as he looks at the beauty of Bee's body and her hair from the back, as it turns into a wonderful sparkling rainbow of colour. Moments later, to delight Wire, she returns to his favourite beautiful blue body with the bright white hair, which makes him think to himself how alluring she is.

Bee opens the upper exit door of the tunnel to get outside onto the surface, where their spacecraft is ready and fully equipped with all they need to escape from Titan moon.

Wire enters the spacecraft first, expecting Bee to follow — but she doesn't. Instead she closes and locks the door from the outside, making Wire wonder why she not got in with him…

*Wire:* 'What are you doing, Bee? Why did you lock the door from the outside and didn't come in here with me?'

She says, while artificial tears flow from her eyes:

*Bee:* 'I can't escape with you, my beloved Wire.'

*Wire:* 'Why?'

*Bee:* 'My operating system is controlled by a Mother Company device. As soon as I leave the atmosphere of Titan moon, my system dies automatically, forever.'

Desperately he replies with a feeling of extreme anxiety that he may never see her again:

*Wire:* 'I can't believe what you are saying! Please do something and run away with me, otherwise The Mother Company will shut you down!'

*Bee:* 'Do you remember how to operate the spacecraft? All you have to do is to speak up and choose the moon or the planet that you would like to travel to.'

As tears appear from his eyes for the first time…

*Wire:* 'This is unbelievable! Please come with me, Bee.'

*Bee:* 'I have to close the tunnel door now, otherwise The Mother Company will

>            terminate me. Goodbye, Wire! I love
>            you.'

Bee slams the tunnel door shut, and Wire is shocked with confusion and disbelief.

*Wire:*         'What should I do? Where should I go?'

The spacecraft replies, thinking that Wire was asking a question:

*Spacecraft:*   'Welcome to the spacecraft! Please select the moon or the planet destination from this solar system that is suitable for your kind…

                'Moons: Europa, Callisto, Ganymede or Io.

                'Planets: Mars or Earth.'

Wire thought to himself, 'I have always been taught about the beauty of planet Earth by Bee, and how life used to be amazing on there before the machines enslaved humans, and the fatal asteroid collision. I will choose planet Earth.' He shouts, 'EARTH!!!'

*Spacecraft:*   'Thank you for choosing planet Earth. The average temperature is appropriate for a human being to live. The journey will take at least four years in Earth time, and the distance is one million, two hundred thousand kilometers. Thank you and have a pleasant journey.'

The spacecraft starts to take off and Wire's tears started streaming again, in the knowledge that his departure would mean he would never see Bee again.

Wire sits and looks at the glassy ground floor contemplating his situation, shocked by what Bee has done to him. He never believed she would sacrifice her life for him. He is overwhelmed by her courage and bravery.

Wire speaks aloud to himself, 'Why did you do all this for me? I think today I just realized the meaning of the word "love".'

He eagerly glances back to the spacecraft door, hoping he will see Bee one more time so he can wave goodbye. But she is not there, and all he sees is the depressing sight of Titan moon from a short distance, with robots creating each other in a large pyramid style building. It is showing very strange drawings and various shapes, and at the top of the pyramid is an unusual light colour (to the human eye). He assumes that it is The Mother Company; but there is no sign of Bee.

Moments later, Titan moon disappears and any hope of seeing Bee again disappears with it. Through exhaustion and heartbreak at this stage, he falls into a deep sleep.

# The Journey

Strange voices, a crying baby, fast footsteps, strange images, shapes and drawings, a shy bird looking like the hoopoe bird with a magical sound coming out of its beak, turning from a bird into a snake and then from a snake to a whale, a huge explosion in dense deep water, a very bright moon light on a cold desert resembling the surface of Titan, a voice calling him, echoing 'I love you, Wire,' and another frightening voice commanding to shut her system down permanently — he wakes up from his nightmare with sweat pouring out from his forehead, heart beating heavily, imagining what The Mother Company has done to Bee.

Days go by, and all he does is drink, eat and sleep with no idea of how long he has been in this spacecraft. He contemplates the universe, seeing nothing else apart from darkness and the magnificence of its beautiful stars. It makes him wonder, 'What is this space that has no end? This great universe, where did it all come from? Who made it, and who created my own kind? How was life on Earth long before the machines enslaved humans? And where did humans come from? I feel like I have been imprisoned within this universe and not just inside my spacecraft! Why can't I choose what I want in life? Why can't I see Bee again? I must stop thinking, otherwise I will go crazy.'

Time passes, the spacecraft announces that they are now passing by planet Saturn, Wire wakes up from his sleep and looks from the spacecraft's transparent surrounding wall, to see this giant sparkling planet with its stunning, golden, icy rings circling around in one level—adding a magical touch to its beauty, with many moons around it.

This amazing sight takes his breath away, and he says to himself, 'I wish Bee were with me now to share this moment. Who made all this? No way the machines did all this, so who did?'

A year has passed since he has seen Saturn. The spacecraft speaks again, and says they are now passing alongside the planet Jupiter. Wire looks at this huge planet and compares it to Saturn with its many moons, making him wonder if there is any life on this planet? It is so much bigger than Saturn with its white, red, orange, brown and yellow colours that blend with each other, making it so unique for its kind.

The spacecraft speaks again after another year, announcing that they are now passing by the planet Mars. Wire again looks out of the transparent wall in the same way he did when he saw Saturn and Jupiter. He sees a red planet — this time with only two moons. This makes him wonder yet again, 'Why does every planet have a different colour? Why does this planet have only two moons, but Jupiter and Saturn have over a hundred moons?

Are these planets connected in some way? Do they speak to each other? How can these giant worlds stand still in space without leaning on anything but just dark space? I am tired of all the questions I have, and no one is answering them for me. Will I find the answers when I get to Earth?'

After four years of a journey that has never been achieved by mankind, the spacecraft speaks, 'We are approaching planet Earth!'

Wire jumps for joy from the amazement of what he has heard at last, and says to himself, 'Finally! I have waited long enough for this moment to see the planet that Bee always talked about.'

His eyes smile with a wide-open mouth from the fascination of seeing planet Earth. It's predominantly blue with white plumes, reminding him of his beloved Bee's blue body and her sparkling white hair.

'What a beautiful planet! It is really beautiful! I'm going to name it planet Bee. But no! No! It must remain being called planet Earth. What will I find on it? And what a waste—I'm going to live on this planet just by myself! Well at least I will live without The Mother Company's restrictions. If only Bee was with me right now.'

The spacecraft is approaching the surface of Earth, and Wire remembers what Bee did for him to reach this moment. He says to himself, 'Bee, I will never forget your love and the sacrifice you made for me.'

The spacecraft breaks into the clouds and decreases its speed…

Countdown begins: 10−9−8−7−6−5−4−3−2−1−Zero!

*Spacecraft:* 'We have landed safely on planet Earth. The temperature is moderate and stable for a human being. I hope you had a pleasant journey and thank you.'

The spacecraft door opens, and Wire is finding it difficult to move. The muscles in his body are weakened due to the lack of gravity, and his inability to feel his own weight in space since the day he was born. Even though his eyes are not used to the sunlight, he still takes his helmet off, hesitating to breathe the natural oxygen of planet Earth for the first time. He comes out crawling onto the sand, his hands feeling the sea and tasting its salty water, which gives him a mixed feeling that combines laughing and crying at the same time. He is happy in the knowledge that he has reached planet Earth but devastated for leaving Bee behind back on Titan moon, not knowing her destiny.

He rolls over on to his back and the gentle waves hit his face. This makes him look at the clear blue sky, while seeing his spacecraft disappearing out of sight. Soon afterwards, he passes out.

# The Island

Strange noises wake him. He opens his eyes to see human-like figures with long hair and dark complexion. They are all wearing and carrying bones that have sharp ends. They follow each other in a circle around him, some surprised, some happy to see him, while some are crying with hysteria. They light a fire around him and start dancing.

Wire tries to open his eyes again, thinking he is still sleeping in a dream; but soon he realizes that he is in a true world of reality, shocked by finding himself being restrained. He tries to talk to them in his native numeric Titan moon language which they do not understand, and they completely ignore him.

Wire thinks, 'What are these creatures that resemble me? Are they just human like me but looking so different? If they are humans, how did they survive on the surface of Earth after the asteroid collision? How come there is still life here? I thought I would be alone! At least I know now that I am not by myself on this planet.'

They carry Wire to their residence and put him in front of an elderly man who is surrounded by many of his followers. Wire guesses that he is their leader. They start whispering, and the elderly man speaks to everyone. While Wire doesn't understand anything, the man starts inspecting Wire by using his forefinger, prodding various parts of his upper body. Then he looks at Wire's bright blue eyes with a stunned expression on his face. He raises both hands to the sky and points them to the Sun, shouting in excitement, making everyone scream and cry while their hands are also drawn towards the Sun.

Suddenly a figure jumps out of the crowd and attempts to strangle Wire with his hands, but guards prevent him and pull him away. Then their leader speaks again and commands the guards to lock Wire in a wooden cage, leaving him with some milk and a piece of meat that resembles a human arm. They untie him and set him free in the cage.

Wire starts crying and says, 'I didn't come to Earth to be put in a cage! I have been imprisoned for long enough on Titan moon, you can't do this to me, I want to be free!'

He looks around and sees others locked in cages. They are all looking at him astonished, as if they have seen a ghost. He tries to speak to them, but they are unable to communicate with him, so he starts drinking the milk while looking at the piece of meat that was brought to him. He gets disgusted by the blood leaking from what looks like an arm, so he kicks it away with his foot, then retreats into a corner and falls asleep.

In the middle of the night, while everyone is asleep, the guards come back again to take one individual from the cage next to Wire. He looks terrified and starts screaming and crying. You can tell from his body language that he is pleading for mercy. They tie him up while they are singing, then they take him to the middle of the surrounding circle and throw him to the ground in front of their leader. They lift up a huge rock and smash it against his head to break the skull. He dies immediately, and they pierce the chest with a sharp bone to extract the heart while it's still beating.

With blood flowing from his hand, one of the followers presents it to their leader, who then takes a bite from the heart and throws the remains to his followers, leaving them each fighting for a share. Then they light more fire around the dead body while cutting it into pieces, roasting each piece to eat, making Wire and the prisoners petrified of the possible fate that awaits them.

They offer Wire a piece of the roasted meat but Wire refuses and vomits, shocked from what he has seen. He says, 'You are not humans, you are monsters! You are worse than the machines! How could you eat your own people? Who would you eat next? Please, let me go!'

Next morning cold water is poured onto his face. That wakes him from his deep sleep. It's a beautiful girl, carrying with her a leather skin displaying symbols and shapes. The guards open the wooden cage door, letting him free. She waves at him to follow her. He obeys, and they approach the leader. She acknowledges the leader with a nod. Then she tries to speak with Wire to teach him their own language, so they can communicate. Wire understands and agrees to learn.

They never harm Wire — in fact, they look after him. Every day, the girl keeps teaching Wire their language, and with time Wire begins to understand their customs and traditions, including the wearing of leaves from the local trees to blend in.

Time passes by, and one day while they are on the beach together, while Wire is practising some words, he tries to explain to the girl where he came from by grabbing her hand and pointing to the moon. He attempts to explain that he came from a world that is similar to Earth's moon, but she gets confused and shakes her head disagreeing. Then she grabs his hand like the way he did to her and directs it towards the Sun, looking at his eyes and lips. She kisses him, then gently pulls away to explain that her father is the leader of the tribe.

*The Girl:* 'My father told all the tribes on the island that you are a messenger sent from our God, the Sun — the God we worship. You are a prophet of the Sun, and you are here to save us from an unknown enemy.'

*Wire:* 'This is not true. I did not come from the Sun; I came from a moon called Titan. Can I ask you a question? Why do you eat each other?'

*The Girl:* 'We don't eat each other; we only eat our enemies who attack us from time to time. There are other tribes that live with us on this island. We cooperate with most of them, but not all — the ones in the cages are currently our enemies. We eat them to strengthen

> our bodies and hearts, so we become strong and fearless.'

*Wire:* 'So why wasn't I eaten?'

*The Girl:* 'I told you, we only eat our enemies, and you are not one of them. You are our prophet. You are different from us—we know that by the way you look. If we eat you, our God the Sun will become very angry and leave us, sending heavy rainstorms and diseases to torture us.'

They kiss again, but this time for longer, until Wires stops to ask her:

*Wire:* 'What's your name?'

*The Girl:* 'My name is Aponi, given to me by my father; it means butterfly. What about you?'

He starts smiling, and says,

*Wire:* 'My name is Wire. It means a metal in the form of a thin flexible thread or rod. A physical wire path can transmit a specific signal or physical energy.

|            | It's usually found in electronic devices. I don't think you will understand the meaning of my name!' |
| --- | --- |
| *Aponi:* | 'A very strange name that has many meanings. You are truly a prophet from our God the Sun. I'm so thankful you have been sent to us!' |

She looks towards the Sun and starts praying after Wire explains his name. Wire starts looking around the island, seeing all the swaying trees dancing, giant mountains and different varieties of eye-catching animals. Looking at the sheer beauty of its nature with the sounds of birds singing, makes him think to himself what a beautiful planet Earth is. Bee was right. Earth is the place to be. Earth is the best place in the Universe!

Wire gets used to their lifestyle and starts speaking their language fluently. He marries Aponi, and the tribe present them with a jar full of golden liquid to share together as a wedding gift. Wire hesitates, but Aponi nods her head, insisting for him to try it first. He dips his finger in and licks it nervously, only to find that he loves the flavour. He asks Aponi,

*Wire:*       'This is delicious — what is it?'

*Aponi:*     'We call this "honey". During our tribal ceremony we are allowed to have honey only on this special day, meaning that only today the two of us can enjoy the taste of honey.'

He smiles, and immediately remembers Bee when she used to tell him all about the benefits of honey. But he hides the memory from Aponi, and continues enjoying the moment, tasting this wonderful honey as if no one had ever told him about it before.

After their marriage, they have a baby, naming her Bee. Soon after, he asks their leader to bring everyone together, so he can announce an important message. This is agreed, and the news spreads all over the island over that day. As people were believing he might tell them a message from their God the Sun, almost everyone comes and gathers together to hear what their prophet would say. Wire stands and speaks:

*Wire:* 'People of the island, after learning your own customs and traditions, and now able to speak your language fluently, it is time for me to tell you all the truth.'

He pauses for a moment and speaks again:

*Wire:* 'My name is Wire, and I'm not a messenger or a prophet who came from the Sun. I have come from a moon named Titan, similar to your moon. I have escaped from an evil machine, an organization called The Mother Company. A robot who worked for them loved me deeply and helped me to escape. Her name was Bee; she sacrificed her life for me, and without her I would have died.

A long time ago, millions of years ago, human beings became advanced in science and technology. They made machines that were able to think just like humans, and with time the machines' artificial intelligence developed itself and enslaved all mankind. They ruled planet Earth and destroyed anything that tried to control them.

They are so smart that they can carry out any task given to them, and much more. They use a language based on algorithms. All machines speak it on Titan moon, and with it they can create each other and do what is impossible for us humans to do. They left just before an asteroid collision with Earth that destroyed all living species. They took five hundred eggs of human genes to Titan moon, where they were born and raised by The Mother Company.

After they had studied and learnt everything about our emotions and

> behaviors, we were of no use anymore, so they decided to kill all of us—all the five hundred! Only I managed to escape; the rest are dead. Your beliefs and religion are wrong. The Sun is a burning star, just like the other stars you see in the sky, and planet Earth is round, not flat like you believe. I have seen this with my own eyes before landing here.'

People start whispering, confused by what Wire is saying.

*The Leader:* 'Enough! Wire, what are you talking about?'

*Wire:* 'I'm speaking the truth, my leader.'

*The Leader:* 'No, you are not! You are a prophet sent by our God the Sun, I wonder if you have been drinking too much today, or you are losing your mind!'

*Wire:* 'I'm fully aware of what I'm saying. It's the truth, and I haven't been drinking.'

*The Leader:*   'Silence!'

People started laughing, making fun out of Wire's story, thinking he is crazy. Observing their response, he leaves them and runs away towards the beach. He had waited all this time for this moment to tell them—but they couldn't see the truth, as they didn't believe him.

He stands in front of the sea, looking at its flowing waves. He remembers Bee, when she used to tell him all about the ocean, from its reflective sky colour to the wonderful variety of fish swimming freely in it; but he never believed her and now everyone else doesn't believe him.

This triggers a question in his mind to which he has never had an answer. Speaking to himself, he says, 'Bee has told me that, millions of years ago, an asteroid collision destroyed planet Earth and killed all mankind. The machines left before this disastrous event to survive, taking with them five hundred human gene eggs—including my own. So how did all this happen, and all I see is the opposite? Life is completely normal here! Humans, animals, trees, seas and rivers still exist. I cannot see any evidence of the collision. How come Bee told me all this? It doesn't make any sense. Am I really crazy, as all the people on the island think? Or did Bee get confused with another planet?'

Years pass by, and Wire becomes an old man. He had forgotten where he came from and carries on with his life just like the others on the island. As he approaches the last few days of his life, one day while he was lying on a hammock near his home a young girl comes towards him, running fast, very fast. Her eyes are wide open and terrified, like she has seen death in front of her. She stops and speaks with a broken voice,

*Young Girl:* 'There … are … very …'

*Wire:* 'Little girl, stop! Take a deep breath and start again.'

*Young Girl:* 'There are very large boats approaching our island. We are going to have more prophets. My grandmother told me they will arrive, and this day has come.'

*Wire:*        'Girl, what are you talking about?'

*Young Girl:*  'Everyone is on the beach watching the large boats. Come with me — I will show you.'

He attempts to run after her but is unable to, as he is old, and all he can do is to try to walk fast. Suddenly they hear a very loud whistle that they have never heard before. The sound feels like a warning coming from the seashore side. With trees blocking his view, he carries on walking to find out the unknown. He arrives on the shore and sees what his eyes have never witnessed before.

Huge ships are there, larger than all their own small boats. They are made from a solid material, with people on board looking like himself. His eyes blink rapidly trying to see clearly what's in front of him. He sees small boats hanging down from the large ships, and now they are heading to the coast of the island with red boxes — rectangular in shape. All the people of the island are shocked by what they are seeing, and everyone starts praying, thanking their God the Sun for sending them more prophets. All except Wire; he is the only one who knows they did not come from the Sun, but he doesn't know from where.

The first boat arrives on to the beach, with one of the sailors holding a red box in his hand trying to speak into it. He says:

*The Sailor:* 'Hello, my name is Leo. We are an exploration team to islands that have no connection with our modern world. We are here only to make friends with you and to learn about your culture, we are people just like you, We have plenty of gifts — like fruit, vegetables, clean water — and we can also provide health care to everyone.'

Another shock to the people of the island: a loud voice coming from this red box speaking their language! For them it's like some magic, but Wire understands that it's a tool to translate between them. But he still can't figure out where these sailors have come from.

As Wire approaches them, slowly, Leo and his team look at him. They are very surprised at seeing Wire amongst the people of the island, because of his distinctive appearance. Leo starts speaking again without using the red box, thinking that Wire can understand him; but Wire could not, so he speaks again through the red box:

*Leo:* 'What is your name, and where are you from?'

*Wire:* 'My name is Wire, and I came from Titan moon.'

Leo and his team are puzzled, so he asked again,

Leo: 'What is your name and where are you from?'

*Wire:* 'I told you my name is Wire, and I have escaped from Titan moon.'

Leo's team started smiling.

*Leo:* 'How long have you been on this island?'

*Wire:* 'Since I was a young man.'

*Leo:* 'Do you speak English? Can you speak any other language apart from your island one?'

*Wire:* 'Yes I do, I speak the language of Titan moon, the language of algorithm.'

Leo's face looked on with sadness after Wire replies. From Leo's eyes, Wire can read that he is feeling sorry for him.

*Leo:* 'I think you have been on this island for many years. As a result, you have become sick and need a psychiatrist. We can provide a doctor to check your health and give you treatment.'

*Wire:* 'I'm not sick! I'm telling you the truth.'

*Leo:* 'Would you like to come with us?'

*Wire:* 'To where?'

*Leo:* 'To our country. It's a different land from your island. We can provide you with everything you need.'

*Wire:* 'What about my family?'

*Leo:* 'They can come with you too.'

*Wire:* 'What about the people of the island?'

*Leo:* 'They can also come — but in different ships, for safety reasons.'

*Wire:* 'Do not worry. The people of the island are peaceful. They only harm those who attack them.'

*Leo:* 'Okay, we trust you.'

# United Kingdom

Wire and his family get on board in one of the large iron ships, heading towards the unknown land. Ten days later, they arrive in the country called Great Britain—specifically at Greenwich docks, in the city of London. Large crowds of people gather to see this tribe that has been isolated for thousands of years. Countless news media, local and global, come to record and interview them. Everyone wants to see the tribe and especially Wire who had been found with them on the island.

When they arrive, the press cameras are continuously shooting photographs without stopping. The flashlight makes Wire and his family use their arms to cover their eyes — it's very bright for them. Leo already briefed them that this could happen, so they understand; but they are still bothered by it. The questions start firing from all the journalists who are fighting over Wire and his family to get answers.

'Sir, what's your name?'

'Do you speak English?'

'Where are you from?'

'Are you from the UK?'

'What is your religion?'

'How did you end up on the island?'

'Would you say something, please?'

As the press flood them with questions, there is no response, as Wire and his family do not speak the English language. The police try to protect them from harassment, so they drive them away to a building for the purpose of housing and investigation. All this is done under the supervision of the British Government.

On the journey, Wire and his family are shocked by everything they are witnessing around them—vehicles, traffic lights, buildings, electronic devices, noise, peoples' clothes and their hairstyle. But what is more surprising to Wire, is that an old question is triggered in his mind—the question to which never had an answer. He speaks to himself, 'Why did Bee tell me that an asteroid destroyed planet Earth, with everything moving on it? Why would she tell me this, and life looks completely fine here? Was she wrong, or am I an old man who has started going crazy and imagining things?'

The next day, the hearings investigation committees' team, through the red box translation tool, start asking Wire questions. They aim to find out who is he and how he ended up being on the island, but with no results. Each time, they ask him about his name, and where he originally came from before he travelled to the island. He repeats the same answer, saying that he came from Titan moon, and his name is Wire.

They have no records of him, and they get tired of trying. So, they refer Wire to a psychiatrist, who applies psychiatric session treatments and gives him some tablets. They did not believe his story, and conclude he is mentally ill with schizophrenia. They think he became like this as a result of trauma that he has experienced when he survived from some form of danger. They couldn't extract any information from him, but they believed he may have originated from Europe or North America.

A few days later, the investigations continue via the red box translation tool. This time they brought the most senior investigator in the country, who starts by introducing himself…

*Investigator:* 'My name is Peter, and I'm here to interview you. The point of this meeting is just to help you, Mr. Wire. Do you understand me?'

*Wire:* 'Yes.'

*Peter:* 'Okay, I will start my questions. What's your name?'

*Wire:* 'My name is Wire.'

*Peter:* 'Okay Wire, what's your full name?'

*Wire:* 'What do you mean?'

| | |
|---|---|
| *Peter:* | 'What's your surname, or your father's name?' |
| *Wire:* | 'I don't know.' |
| *Peter:* | 'How old are you?' |
| *Wire:* | 'I do not know.' |
| *Peter:* | 'Where were you born, what country?' |
| *Wire:* | 'I was born on Titan moon.' |
| *Peter:* | 'Ha Ha! I think you are a funny man, Mr. Wire.' |
| *Wire:* | 'Am I?' |
| *Peter:* | 'Let's move on. What's your religion?' |
| *Wire:* | 'What do you mean by the word "religion"?' |
| *Peter:* | 'I meant; do you believe in God? What's your belief? For example, I'm a Christian, and I believe Jesus is the son of God. There are other religions too, such as Islam, Judaism, Buddhism and Hinduism. So, which one do you belong to?' |
| *Wire:* | 'Do I have to belong to one?' |

*Peter:* 'Not really, but most people do.'

*Wire:* 'Sorry, but I still do not understand what you mean by the word "religion". But if you meant it is like how the people of the island worship the Sun, then I do not believe in such a thing.'

*Peter:* 'Okay then, you must be a non-believer. Let's move on. So, do you know what date it is, or the day today?'

*Wire:* 'I do not understand.'

*Peter:* 'Do you realize we are in the year 2020?'

*Wire:* 'No.'

*Peter:* 'Do you know the meaning of your name Wire, in the English language?'

*Wire:* 'No, I don't know in the English language, but I know that in Titan moon's language it means a path that transmits a specific physical signal or an energy.'

| | |
|---|---|
| *Peter:* | 'That's correct, that's the definition of Wire in the English language.' |
| *Wire:* | 'This is odd! How come my name comes from your culture? It's The Mother Company on Titan moon who gave me this name.' |
| *Peter:* | 'I will ask you more later about The Mother Company, but for now can you please tell me how you travelled from Titan moon to Earth?' |
| *Wire:* | 'In a Spacecraft. Bee built it for me, so I could escape from Titan moon.' |
| *Peter:* | 'Your daughter, Bee?' |
| *Wire:* | 'No not my daughter Bee — I'm talking about a different person on Titan moon, also named Bee. She is a machine — a robot, not a human. She sacrificed her life for me so I could escape from the Mother Company.' |

The senior investigator Peter, realises he is not able to progress further with the investigation, so he replies,

*Peter:* 'Okay, I think this is enough for today. I'm going to stop the investigation and close your file until you finish your psychiatric treatment sessions and you get better. I think you should follow up with your doctor and continue taking your medications. Thank you.'

Wire is saddened by the responses of all the people he has met. Everyone thinks he is mentally ill. No one wants to believe him, just as the people of the island never did. So, he decides to get on with his life again.

Britain grants him and his family a residency in their land. He starts learning English to cope with his new life, while his daughter Bee enters a school. All this new busy life does not make him forget what Bee has told him on Titan moon, that the machines enslaved mankind, and an asteroid collided with the Earth, destroying everything on its surface. Still, today he is not sure why Bee would tell him false information, when everything looks so normal on planet Earth?

One day, while he was spending time on his daily routine visiting the library, reading and researching the books of the famous scientist Albert Einstein, Wire discovers the theories of relativity, the speed of light and wormholes. He finds out that time is a relative illusion and not a fact; that it varies according to the speed of light through space. He thinks that time and space are part of one thing. With this speed of light through the wormholes, we can race with time and travel to the future or to the past. This opens his mind to conclude that the machines—with their artificial intelligence—can travel at the speed of light to millions of years into the future or to the past in Earth time.

He started telling himself... 'Bee built a spacecraft for me to travel from Titan moon to planet Earth. It wasn't just an ordinary spacecraft, but rather it was a vehicle to travel through time. It took me into a beautiful era that Bee always loved. All those years that passed while I was in the spacecraft must have been in another time dimension. The stars and the planets with their moons that I saw while I was travelling were just an illusion. Was it a trick by Bee to convince me I was going to Earth, without telling me it was into their past? Because our human minds cannot accommodate the idea of travelling into the past, otherwise we would have the ability to change events that have already happened. That contradicts with the rules of physics! She gave me the option to travel to any planet or moon, but she knew I would choose planet Earth. She knew that because she had told me so much about its beauty. Yes, I must have returned to the past, so the asteroid has not yet collided with the surface of planet Earth! And yes, the machines have not yet enslaved mankind!'

He kept repeating, 'I went back to the past … I went back to the past …'Then he stopped to say, 'Am I going mad, or am I already an old mad man, as the British and the people of the island think?

He returns home with his mind spinning on discovering that he has travelled into the past, and he tells his wife,

*Wire:* 'I need to tell you that I have come from the future.'

*Aponi:* 'What?'

*Wire:* 'As I have told you.'

She rolls her eyes and replies…

*Aponi:* 'Have you taken your tablets this morning?'

He shakes her by her shoulders and looks into her eyes to tell her,

*Wire:* 'Yes I did, but you need to believe me when I say that I have returned to the past! Why you never believe anything that I say? I'm not mad, I'm telling you the truth.'

He leaves her, and heads to central London. He arrives at Oxford Street during a very busy time and stands in the middle where he begins shouting at people — warning them about the intelligence of the machines and the asteroid that will collide with

Earth. But no one is listening to him. Everyone is ignoring him, apart from the angry drivers whose way through he is blocking.

Every day, Wire keeps warning people, but as usual he is being constantly ignored. One day, he comes across a quote in a local newspaper by a scientist named Edward Taylor: "Artificial Intelligence is the best thing has ever happened to human beings. It's going to revolutionize us, and we should keep developing the technology." After Wire reads this, he becomes angry and starts searching the internet for Edward Taylor's name. He finds out that Taylor is a professor, teaching computer science at Oxted University. Wire prints the professor's picture and leaves his house in a rage.

He buys a train ticket and heads to Oxted City, then to its prestigious University, where he asks at the information desk about Edward Taylor.

*Wire:* 'I'm looking for Edward Taylor.'
*Receptionist:* 'He is busy right now giving a lecture to his students. You can come back

|  |  |
|---|---|
|  | later to see him, or we can arrange an appointment for you.' |
| *Wire:* | 'I have an important message to tell him and I must see him right now!' |
| *Receptionist:* | 'It's not allowed! As I said, he is giving a lecture right now. Do you understand me?' |

She gives him a disrespectful look because of his demands. Looking at his scruffy, dirty clothes, she thinks he might be a local vagrant.

| | |
|---|---|
| *Wire:* | 'Yes, I understand you; but my message is more important than his lecture.' |
| *Receptionist:* | 'What's your name then, and what's your message?' |
| *Wire:* | 'My name is Wire, and I have come from the future to warn you all.' |
| *Receptionist:* | 'Okay, I think you should leave. If you don't, I will call security to escort you out of the building.' |

He leaves her and goes to search around the building for the professor. He finds him when looking through a small corridor window and recognises him giving a lecture. He cross-checks with his printed picture before entering the hall full of students. They all look at Wire and wonder who this strange-looking man is that is interrupting their class. Wire nervously asks,

*Wire:* 'Are you Professor Edward Taylor?'

*Professor:* 'Yes, who are you?'

*Wire:* 'My name is Wire. I have travelled from the future, specifically from Titan moon. I need to tell you about the danger of artificial intelligence. The machines will enslave humanity in the near future if you don't stop developing the A.I. technology. You must stop now and put all your focus into how to leave planet Earth before an asteroid wipe all of us out. Instead of developing the A.I. algorithm, you should warn all mankind before it's too late.'

The students burst out laughing at what Wire has said. 'HA! HA! HA!'

*Professor:* 'You come from the future to warn us all, that's great. How about coming back later to continue this, huh?'

*Wire:* 'I'm not coming back later. I have already warned you.'

*Professor:* 'Okay, you have warned us now. Could you please leave my class then?'

*Wire:* 'No, you need to stop teaching A.I. algorithms to your students immediately.'

*Professor:* 'LEAVE NOW!' (shouting).

This infuriates Wire and makes him strike the Professor on the chin with a clenched fist. Security arrive at the class to stop Wire. Then they call the police, who attend to take him away and place him in custody.

The next day Professor Taylor makes an allegation against Wire for assaulting him in front of his students. The authorities discover that Wire has been diagnosed with chronic psychosis, so the court summons him from custody. They sentence him to serve six months in a specialist mental hospital, due to being a danger to himself and to others around him.

Wire is imprisoned in the hospital, and after a long treatment programme with psychiatrists who specialize in mental illness and persevering with taking his tablets at regular intervals, he begins to recover — and realises that he was indeed mentally ill. All his thoughts about the machines, The Mother Company, Titan moon, artificial oxygen, the spacecraft, the island with the people who ate each other, Leo and his exploration team, Peter the investigator, even his family — all of these thoughts were just imaginary and unreal. The only thing that felt real up to now was his love for Bee, even though she never existed.

He gives up on everything, and all he has left is for death to take him away from all the painful psychotic thoughts. He stares from the window of his cell, up into a clear beautiful sunny sky. A buzzing bee enters through a small gap, flies around his bed several times, looking as if it's disturbed and upset from what it senses. Wire opens his palm, signalling for it to land. Then the bee sits on top of his forefinger, he looks at it with tears in his eyes, smiling, remembering the imaginary Bee with her glamorous white hair and enchanting blue body, speaking his last words…

'Goodbye, my honey Bee.'

Two years later, after Wire's death, for the first time the World Aeronautics Space Agency observers detect a burning asteroid, twenty times the size of Mount Everest, heading in the direction of our planet Earth, originating from outside our solar system. They calculate the probability of its collision with planet Earth as 99% certain. Travelling at a speed of 18 kilometres per second, the time of the collision will be sometime in the year 2222.

Another thirty years pass after Wire's death. Robots begin to live with us. We rely on them with almost everything, from cooking and cleaning, to writing the best winning novels or painting the most expensive art. They teach our children, take our dogs for walks, and drive us around safely. But then, and for the first time in mankind, a robot assaults its owner because of cruelty, letting history record the first case of a robot attacking a human being.

In the end, was Wire ever mentally ill? Did he really come from the future, having escaped from Titan moon with the help of Bee, as he claimed? Or was he just a crazy man, who created a silly story for his imaginary love, Bee, just for the love of honey?

# The End

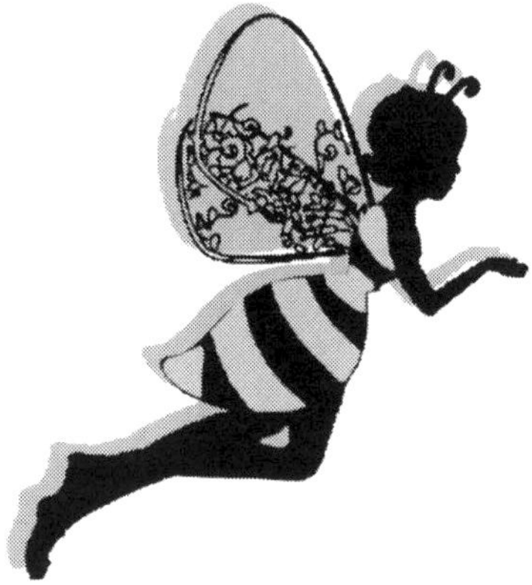

Printed in Poland
by Amazon Fulfillment
Poland Sp. z o.o., Wrocław